LE NOVELLE DELLA CIPOLLA

Matilda Mellor

Homer for Fun
THE ODYSSEY

Text by Cinzia Bigazzi
Illustrations by Celina Elmi

federighi editori

Text by
Cinzia Bigazzi

Illustrations and graphic project by
Celina Elmi

Executive editor
Gloria Pampaloni

Printed by
Federighi Colorgrafiche
50052 Certaldo (Fi)
www.federcol.it

We respect the
environment producing
solar energy

ISBN 978-88-89159-30-9

With **"Homer for Fun - The Odyssey"**,
Homer joins Dante, Boccaccio and Manzoni in
"Le Novelle della Cipolla" series.

The narrative style is well suited for boys and girls of all
ages. The vivid, colourful illustrations will guide readers
through Ulysses' amazing adventures.

Up on the summit of Mount Olympus
the gods were meeting in solemn council.

Up spoke Athena, favourite daughter of Zeus, chief of all the gods: 'Ulysses, the wisest of mortals, has suffered many pains and misadventures, and the nymph Calypso has been holding him captive on the Isle of Ogygia for these past seven years. We *must* help him to get back home to Ithaca! His wife Penelope and his son Telemachus have now been waiting for him for nearly twenty years!' 'Beloved daughter,' Zeus answered, 'remember that Ulysses blinded one-eyed Polyphemus, son of your uncle Poseidon, lord of all the oceans. Ulysses' troubles are Poseidon's revenge.'

'Of course,' Athena nodded. 'But he *had to* put out Polyphemus' eye to save his crew! So let's help him now, before Poseidon comes back from his journey through his seas. Please, send Hermes to Calypso with orders to let Ulysses go! Meanwhile I'll visit Telemachus and prod him into searching for his father.'

Zeus nodded his consent, and Athena, swift as a ray of light, wafted herself down onto Ithaca and there approached Ulysses' palace disguised as Mentes, prince of Taphos. Telemachus greeted her: 'Welcome, oh stranger!' he said, 'Come and sit at our table and tell us of your needs.' The palace was overrun by a horde of arrogant young oafs who were wolfing down piles of food, guzzling wine and roaring out drunken songs. 'These,' Telemachus whispered, 'are rich imbeciles who've come from all over Greece to woo and wed my mother. For four years they've been hanging about every day and night devouring my father's wealth. But if my father were ever to show up again they'd bleat and bolt for the hills like sheep from the wolf, I'll tell you that! But never mind. Tell me who you are, stranger.'

'I'm Mentes, prince of Taphos,' said Athena. **'I've come to tell you that I know your father is alive. Go out and look for him, now!'**

And on that last word she seemed to Telemachus to become an owl and to melt into the air; and he knew suddenly that he had been speaking with a god.

9

The next day Telemachus called an assembly of Ithacan citizens.
'I'm ashamed of and for you,' he berated them loudly. 'You stand by and look away and do nothing whilst these villainous invaders devour the goods and defile the palace and the honour of your king!'
'Oh Telemachus!' Shouted Antinoos, the vilest of the suitors,

'We'd have gone long ago if your mother had chosen one of us! For four years now she's been hoodwinking us with her clever little trick! She promised to decide as soon as she'd done with weaving the shroud for your grandfather Laertes ... but by day she weaves, by night she unravels what she's done, so that nothing can or ever will be finished!'

Just at that instant two eagles sent by Zeus began to wheel and fight in the air above all heads. Aliterxes, wise in the interpretation of the flight of birds cried out 'Silence, everyone! Hear me, oh Ithacans! Ulysses is alive and will be here before long!'

'Shut your silly trap and get out, you stupid old goat!' growled Eurimachus. 'Eurimachus!' shouted Telemachus, 'and all the rest of you! Give me a ship and twenty good men and I'll go and look for my father in Pylos and in Sparta. If he's alive I'll stay away another year, but if I learn that he's dead I'll come back at once and pick a husband for my mother.'

Meanwhile Hermes, messenger of the gods, had arrived on Ogygia.
'Calypso', he said to the nymph, 'I bring orders from Zeus. You are to let Ulysses go. Let him build a raft so that he can sail safely to the Isle of Scheria, home of the Phaecians.'

Calypso was terribly saddened. 'You Olympians are always jealous of the love between a goddess and a mortal! I saved Ulysses from shipwreck, I've kept him safe, sound and loved for seven years, and now you want to take him away from me . . .'

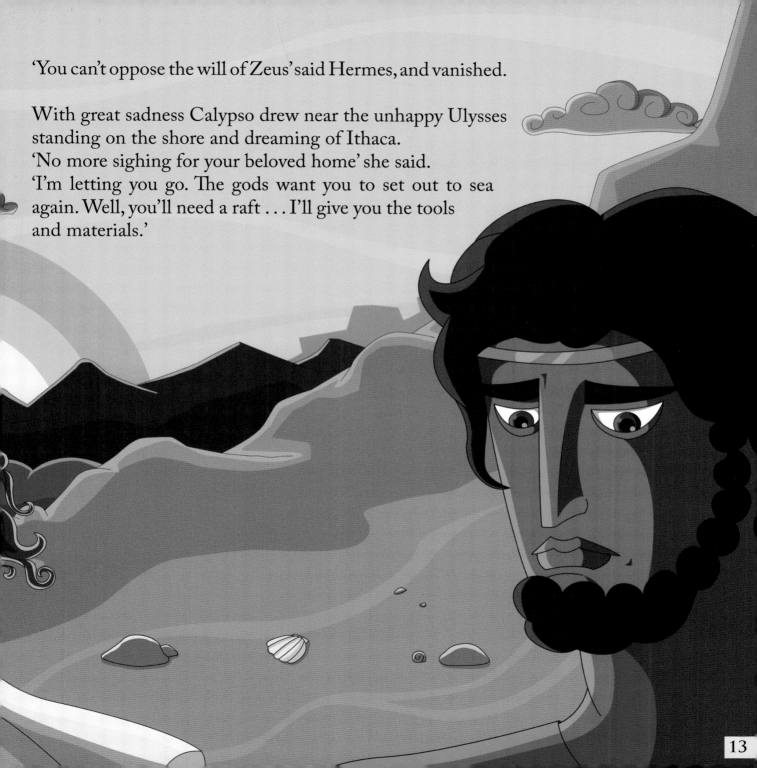

'You can't oppose the will of Zeus' said Hermes, and vanished.

With great sadness Calypso drew near the unhappy Ulysses standing on the shore and dreaming of Ithaca.
'No more sighing for your beloved home' she said.
'I'm letting you go. The gods want you to set out to sea again. Well, you'll need a raft . . . I'll give you the tools and materials.'

Ulysses hardly dared believe his ears: free! After seven years!Five days later the raft was ready and Ulysses set out.

Favourable winds sped him along until, alas!, on the seventeenth day Poseidon returned from his journey to the Ends of the World.

Seeing Ulysses so close to home he fell into a trembling rage: 'So my brethren and sisters on Olympus took advantage of my absence to help Ulysses get back to Ithaca!' he railed. 'Ah, but your voyage isn't over yet, me lad!' – and waving his trident about madly, summoned up a terrible hurricane. A huge wave broke up the raft and tossed Ulysses into the roiling waters.

For two days and two nights he fought desperately for dear life in wild wild seas and was about to go under for good when he heard the sound of breakers on a nearby coast. Soon he felt sand under his feet – **he was safe**!

He dragged himself onto the shore, crawled behind a bush for safety and fell into a long deep sleep. He was awakened by the laughter of a bevy of pretty maidens playing on the beach. Seeing his dishevelled hair, long beard and body all covered in crusts of sea salt they took fright and ran away.

Only one stood firm.
'Please, help me!' Ulysses stammered weakly.
'I'm shipwrecked, I've spent twenty days in storm-tossed seas. . .'.

'You don't look to me like a bad man, stranger,' said the girl, 'and we're peaceful people here. We're the Phaecians. This is the Isle of Scheria, our home. My name is Nausìcaa, and my father, Alcinous, is king.
Follow me – I'll take you to him'.

17

Arrived at the palace, Ulysses was overwhelmed by its beauty and opulence: walls sheathed in bonze, doors of solid gold. He was shown to a bath and a barber and was given new raiment. When he was done and looked well and proper again he was led into the main hall, where a great banquet was taking place.
Bowing deeply before the queen, he said
'My obeisance to your majesty.
I am a shipwrecked wanderer, storm-tossed, sore in body and mind, weary and in need of your help.'

King Alcinous invited him to sit at his side and ordered food and drink for him. When Ulysses had had his fill, entertainment began with a performance by the blind singer and poet Demodocus, who began thus:

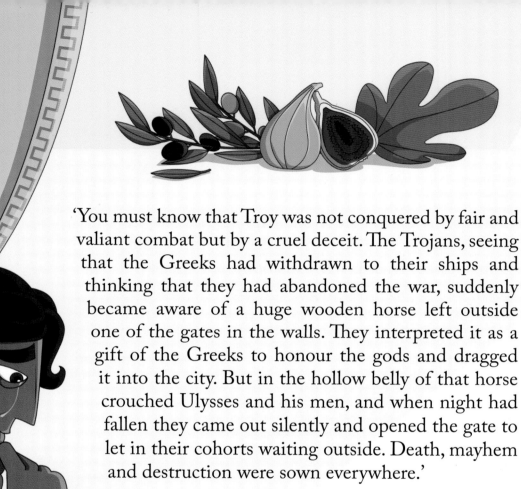

'You must know that Troy was not conquered by fair and valiant combat but by a cruel deceit. The Trojans, seeing that the Greeks had withdrawn to their ships and thinking that they had abandoned the war, suddenly became aware of a huge wooden horse left outside one of the gates in the walls. They interpreted it as a gift of the Greeks to honour the gods and dragged it into the city. But in the hollow belly of that horse crouched Ulysses and his men, and when night had fallen they came out silently and opened the gate to let in their cohorts waiting outside. Death, mayhem and destruction were sown everywhere.'

Hearing these words, Ulysses sighed deeply and tears rolled down his cheeks.
'Who are you, stranger, that the fate of Troy should so move your heart? And where is your home?' Asked Alcinous. 'I,' said Ulysses unsteadily, 'am the inventor of that deceit. **I am Ulysses** . . .' And when the general consternation had calmed down, he added 'And this is my story, if you would be kind enough to hear it . . .'

The war against Troy was over. After ten years of fiercest combat we had won. The city was razed to the ground. All the men and grown youths, including Priam and his sons, had fallen in battle; now the women and children were led off into slavery.

I embarked on one of my twelve ships together with my remaining six hundred men and set sail for Ithaca. After a few days at sea we sighted Ismaros, the city of the Kikones, on the Thracian coast. 'They were traitors!' shouted one of my men. 'They sided with the Trojans!' 'They deserve a lesson!' cried another.

'All right,' I said. 'Let's give them a demonstration of our might.'

After we had sacked and laid waste to Ismaros and divided the rich booty fair and square, my men fell to drunken feasting on the beach. I tried to get them back on the ships and out to sea before the Kikones could rally and muster a revenge attack, but none would listen.

At dawn the Kikones attacked with all their means, and after a gruelling fight we managed, barely, to get off the beaches and away. We lost seventy-two men, six from each one of the twelve ships.

Relieved at our escape but in mourning for our comrades, we re-set our course for home. For two days we were swept along by a steady breeze from astern, but on the third day this changed into a storm.

Zeus, angered by our deeds at Ismaros, asked the wind Boreas to blow up a violent cyclone that shredded our sails to ribbons.

For nine days we drifted at the mercy of the heaving breakers, and only on the tenth could we find refuge in what turned out to be the Isle of the Lotus Eaters. I sent three of the men to scout out the lay of the land, and when after a long time they failed to return we set out in numbers to look for them. We found them in the midst of the lotus-eaters, laughing and having a merry old time!

'Ulysses!' they called out to me, 'Come and try this lovely delicacy: **lotus flowers**! We want to stay here forever . . .'

'Are you crazy?' I cried, 'Have you forgotten about Ithaca?'
'Ithaca?' they said slowly, shaking their heads. 'Oh no. No Ithaca. We love it here, want to stay here . . .' Then I understood: the lotus flower made them forget everything except wanting to stay here forever. I had to kick and whip them back on board and have them tied up in the hold until the effects wore off.
And then I ordered anchors aweigh once again.

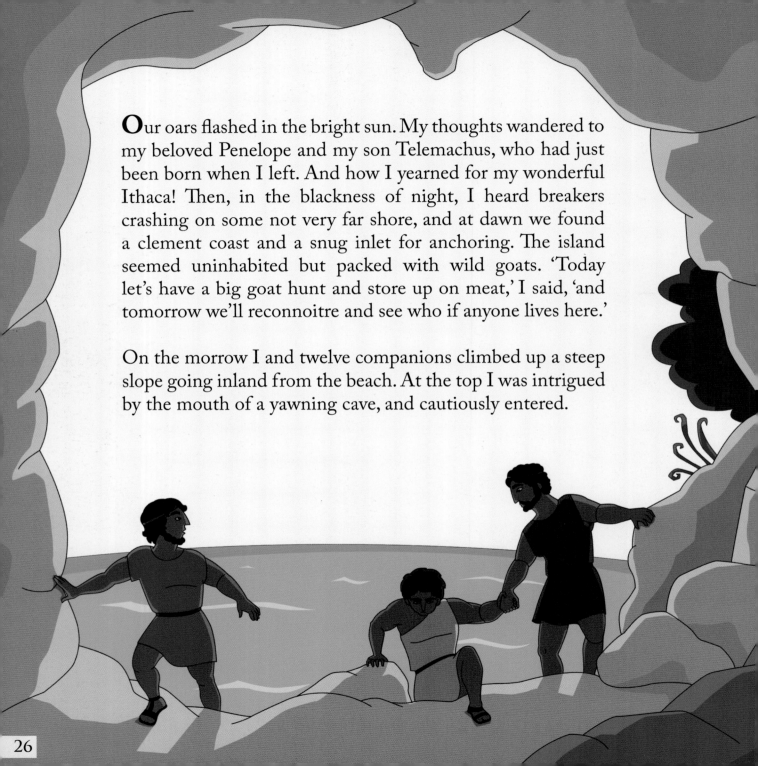

Our oars flashed in the bright sun. My thoughts wandered to my beloved Penelope and my son Telemachus, who had just been born when I left. And how I yearned for my wonderful Ithaca! Then, in the blackness of night, I heard breakers crashing on some not very far shore, and at dawn we found a clement coast and a snug inlet for anchoring. The island seemed uninhabited but packed with wild goats. 'Today let's have a big goat hunt and store up on meat,' I said, 'and tomorrow we'll reconnoitre and see who if anyone lives here.'

On the morrow I and twelve companions climbed up a steep slope going inland from the beach. At the top I was intrigued by the mouth of a yawning cave, and cautiously entered.

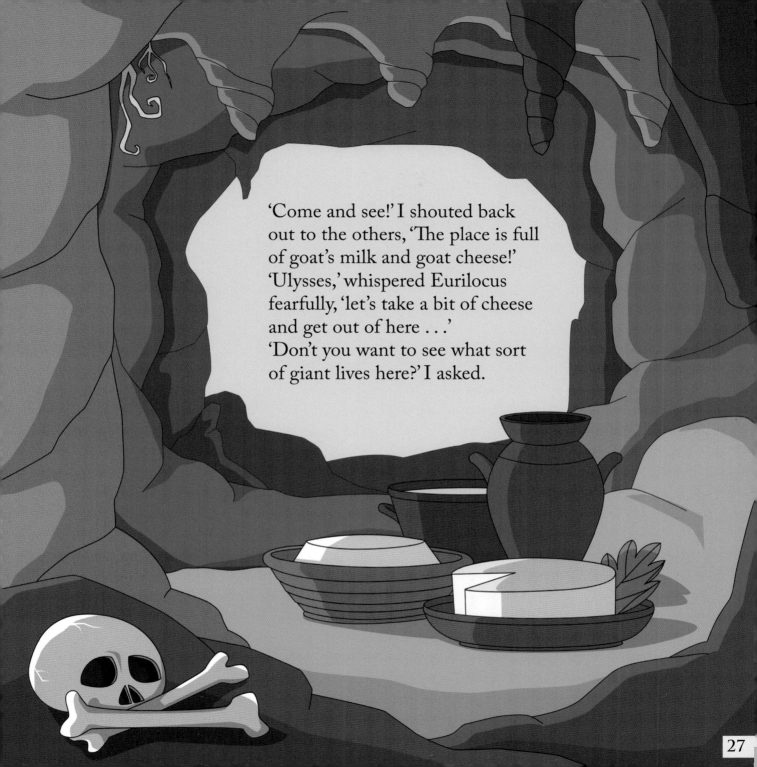

'Come and see!' I shouted back
out to the others, 'The place is full
of goat's milk and goat cheese!'
'Ulysses,' whispered Eurilocus
fearfully, 'let's take a bit of cheese
and get out of here . . .'
'Don't you want to see what sort
of giant lives here?' I asked.

At that moment we heard the bleats of a hundred sheep, and an enormous being appeared at the cave mouth: it was Polyphemus, the one-eyed monstrous giant son of Poseidon. He was huge and all covered in fur, and had but one large eye in the centre of his forehead. Whilst we, terrified, backed off toward the rear of the cave, he let in his sheep and then rolled up a vast boulder to shut the cave from the inside.

When he lit his fire he saw us.

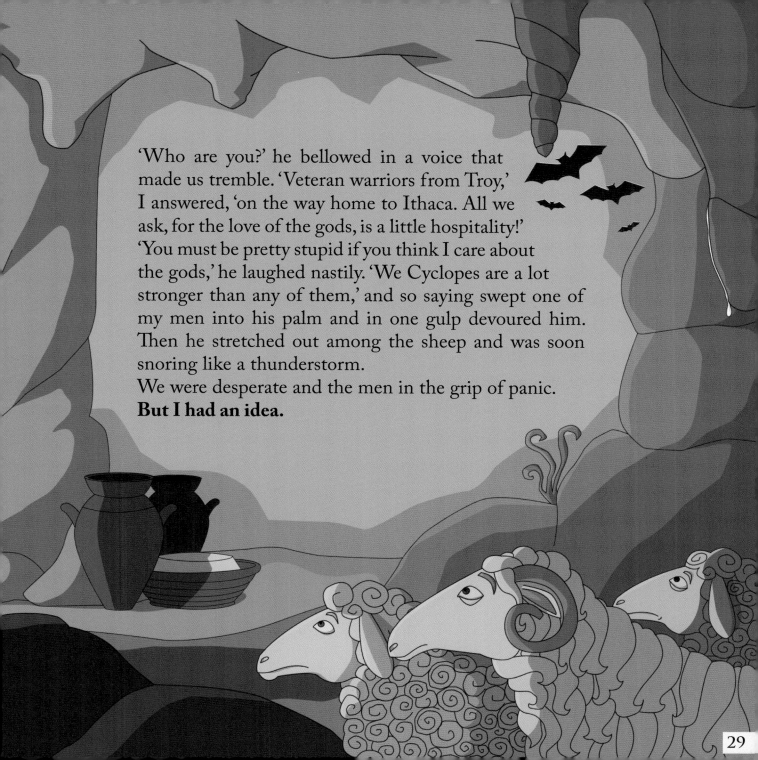

'Who are you?' he bellowed in a voice that made us tremble. 'Veteran warriors from Troy,' I answered, 'on the way home to Ithaca. All we ask, for the love of the gods, is a little hospitality!' 'You must be pretty stupid if you think I care about the gods,' he laughed nastily. 'We Cyclopes are a lot stronger than any of them,' and so saying swept one of my men into his palm and in one gulp devoured him. Then he stretched out among the sheep and was soon snoring like a thunderstorm.

We were desperate and the men in the grip of panic. **But I had an idea.**

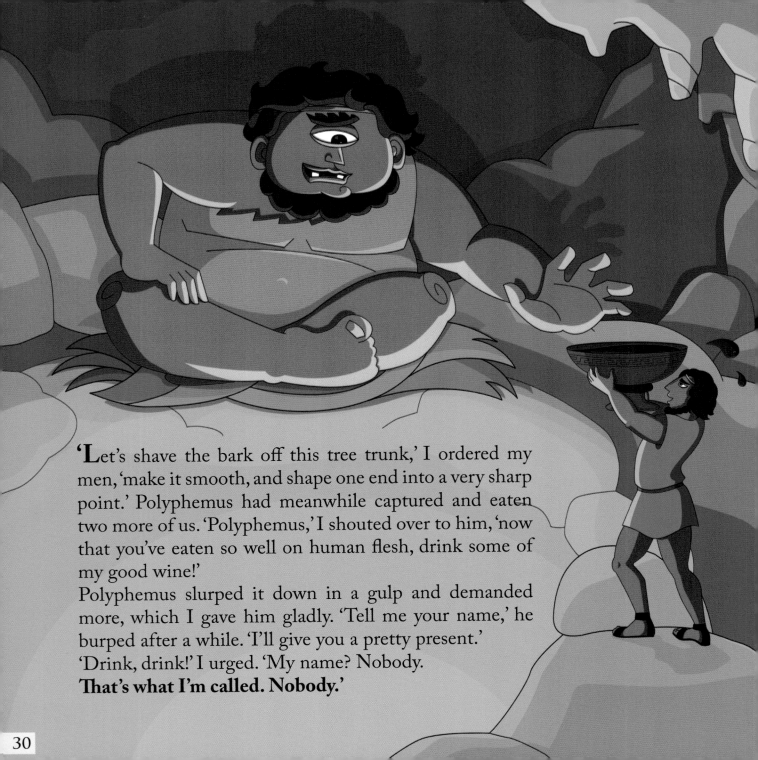

'Let's shave the bark off this tree trunk,' I ordered my men, 'make it smooth, and shape one end into a very sharp point.' Polyphemus had meanwhile captured and eaten two more of us. 'Polyphemus,' I shouted over to him, 'now that you've eaten so well on human flesh, drink some of my good wine!'

Polyphemus slurped it down in a gulp and demanded more, which I gave him gladly. 'Tell me your name,' he burped after a while. 'I'll give you a pretty present.'

'Drink, drink!' I urged. 'My name? Nobody. **That's what I'm called. Nobody.'**

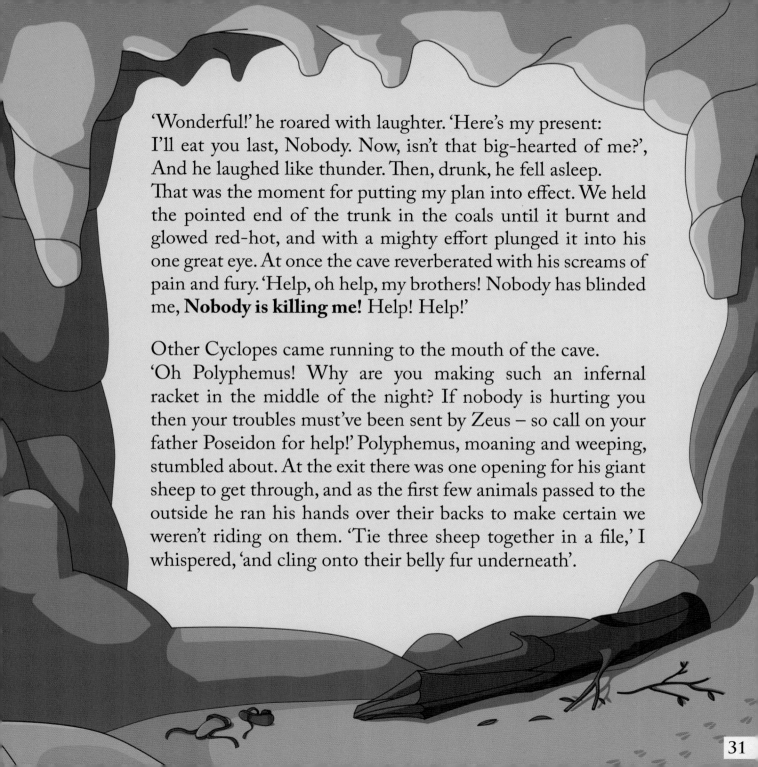

'Wonderful!' he roared with laughter. 'Here's my present: I'll eat you last, Nobody. Now, isn't that big-hearted of me?', And he laughed like thunder. Then, drunk, he fell asleep. That was the moment for putting my plan into effect. We held the pointed end of the trunk in the coals until it burnt and glowed red-hot, and with a mighty effort plunged it into his one great eye. At once the cave reverberated with his screams of pain and fury. 'Help, oh help, my brothers! Nobody has blinded me, **Nobody is killing me!** Help! Help!'

Other Cyclopes came running to the mouth of the cave. 'Oh Polyphemus! Why are you making such an infernal racket in the middle of the night? If nobody is hurting you then your troubles must've been sent by Zeus – so call on your father Poseidon for help!' Polyphemus, moaning and weeping, stumbled about. At the exit there was one opening for his giant sheep to get through, and as the first few animals passed to the outside he ran his hands over their backs to make certain we weren't riding on them. 'Tie three sheep together in a file,' I whispered, 'and cling onto their belly fur underneath'.

I went out last hanging onto the belly fur of a huge ram. Once outside, we ran as fast as we could to our ships, and when we were a ways off shore I shouted back 'Polyphemus! Zeus punished you for having cruelly killed peaceful travellers in search of help. If anyone should ever ask you who it was that blinded you, tell him it was **Ulysses, the destroyer of Troy and king of Ithaca!**

'Ulysses!' screamed Polyphemus. 'It was prophesied that you'd one day blind me, but I expected a huge broad-shouldered mountain of a warrior, not a puny thing like you!' And he picked up one massive stone after another and heaved them into the sea in hopes of sinking us, but missed with all. Then, turning to the Heavens, he cried **'Oh Poseidon, lord and master of the oceans, if you are really my father, punish Ulysses for blinding me! Stop him from ever reaching Ithaca!'** And so we made for the open sea.

Grieving for our six lost mates we arrived at the Isle of Aeolia, where Aeolus, the god of the winds, dwells with his sons and daughters. Aeolus was very hospitable and feasted all my crew for an entire month. At our departure he made me a present of a bloated sheepskin bag well tied shut at the opening. 'Take this gift,' he said. 'In the skin I've imprisoned all he world's winds except one: Zephyrus, whom I left free so that he might speed you on to Ithaca. But never, Ulysses, *never* undo that knot, or you'll be releasing all the unfavourable winds in the world and you'll never see Ithaca again! We sailed on for nine days and nine nights. On the tenth day, by then within sight of the still-distant shores of our beloved Ithaca, I was overcome by fatigue and fell asleep. My mates began to mutter among themselves: 'It's not right that we should come home empty-handed,' growled one, 'whilst Ulysses is laden with riches . . .

34

who knows how much gold and silver Aeolus
gave him in that skin!'. 'Let's open it and see what's in
it' whispered another; and they decided to do it before I could wake
up. When I opened my eyes the knot was already half untied . . . And
all the world's winds were rushing out with a dreadful roar and set up a
hurricane that drove us back out to sea. The men screamed in panic, nor did
I myself know whether to keep to the breaking ship or to leap overboard and
take my chances in the waves. We all clung desperately to beams low in the holds
and tried to survive until the worst of it passed and the seas grew calm again.

We drifted, exhausted, and bewildered, for six days and nights. Early in the morning on the seventh day we made a landfall, far off on the horizon. We beached the ships and I sent men to explore inland. They came running back breathless and terrified almost at once. 'Off, out to sea, quick, quick!' shouted Perimedes, 'it's the land of the horrible giants the Laestrygones! Antiphates their king snatched two of us and ate them then and there!' We raced to the ships and had barely got them afloat when hundreds of Laestrygones came rushing over the crest of the dunes.

Hurling huge boulders, they crushed eleven of the twelve ships – all save mine; and then they skewered to death all the struggling survivors with their long lances. Of the six hundred men who had set out from Troy only forty or so were now left alive.

In my one ship we came to the Isle of Aeaea, home of the sorceress Circe. 'We'll split into two squads,' I ordered. 'One will guard the ship. You, Eurylocus and twenty-two others will go inland and explore.' Soon the explorers had gone far into the forest and come upon the house of the sorceress Circe, who invited them most courteously to come in partake of wine and cheese. All except Eurylocus, who stayed outside, accepted gladly.

What they didn't know was that the food had been bewitched, so that a mere touch from Circe's wand sufficed to turn them all into grovelling pigs that she herded into her pigsties. Eurylocus, weeping and moaning, ran back to the rest of us crying 'Run, into the ships! Away from this accursed place! A beautiful woman has transformed our mates into pigs!'

I rushed into the forest. Just before I came to Circe's palace I was stopped by a young shepherd lad. 'Stop, Ulysses!' he held up his hand. 'I'm Hermes, sent by Zeus. Your men have been turned into swine, and the same will happen to you if you don't eat this herb, called *moly* – **it'll make you immune to Circe's magic.** Eat and drink what she gives you, for when she'll touch you afterward with her wand, nothing will happen to you. Then draw your sword and force her to unbewitch the men and make them human again.' And Hermes vanished into thin air.

I rushed up to the palace. Circe offered me the same magic food. After I had eaten and drunk she touched me with her wand and hissed 'Off to the pigsty with you!' But nothing happened. I drew my sword and brandished it as though to kill her, but she cried out 'What? You don't fall under my spell? Then you must be Ulysses, famed among all men and gods for bravery and astuteness!'

'And so I am,' I said. 'And now, please, free my men and swear that you'll do us no more harm' Circe touched the pigs with her wand and they were themselves again at once. Then she swore to do us no harm and added 'You're all sea-tossed, hungry and weary. Stay here with me – there's food and drink aplenty for you to recover your health and strength!'

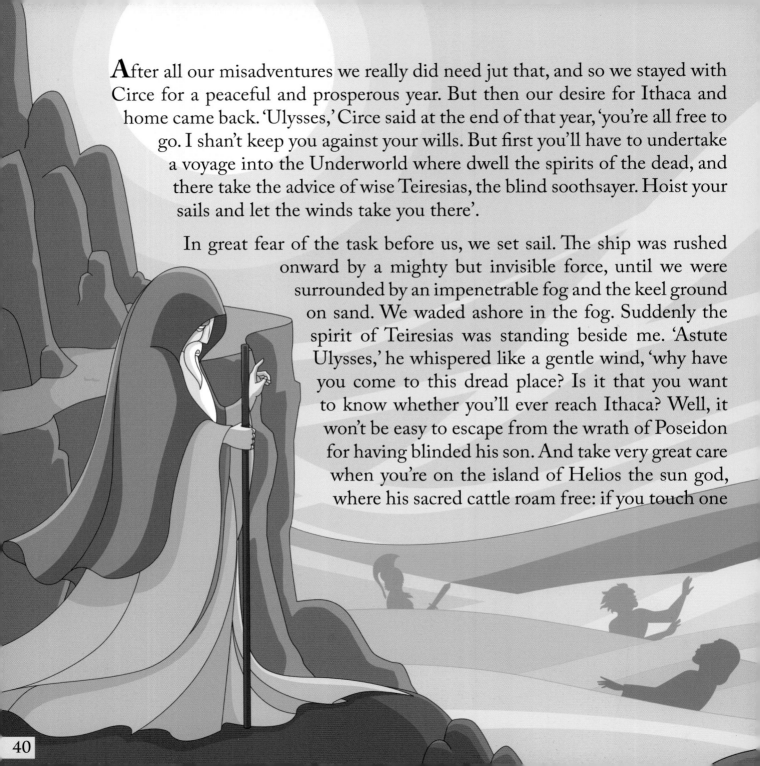

After all our misadventures we really did need jut that, and so we stayed with Circe for a peaceful and prosperous year. But then our desire for Ithaca and home came back. 'Ulysses,' Circe said at the end of that year, 'you're all free to go. I shan't keep you against your wills. But first you'll have to undertake a voyage into the Underworld where dwell the spirits of the dead, and there take the advice of wise Teiresias, the blind soothsayer. Hoist your sails and let the winds take you there'.

In great fear of the task before us, we set sail. The ship was rushed onward by a mighty but invisible force, until we were surrounded by an impenetrable fog and the keel ground on sand. We waded ashore in the fog. Suddenly the spirit of Teiresias was standing beside me. 'Astute Ulysses,' he whispered like a gentle wind, 'why have you come to this dread place? Is it that you want to know whether you'll ever reach Ithaca? Well, it won't be easy to escape from the wrath of Poseidon for having blinded his son. And take very great care when you're on the island of Helios the sun god, where his sacred cattle roam free: if you touch one of them you'll lose your last ship and your last companions. You yourself will manage to survive and reach home, but when you get there you'll find your palace invaded by men who are vying to marry your wife whilst they fatten on your riches and despoil your home. But you'll eventually die peacefully of old age. That, Ulysses, is my prophesy. Now go.' And with that he vanished into the fog.

Suddenly my mother was by my side. 'Mother!' I cried, 'are you, too, dead?' 'I died of grief at the loss of you,' she said, 'but Penelope is still waiting for you!' I reached out to touch her but she melted away like a shadow or a dream.

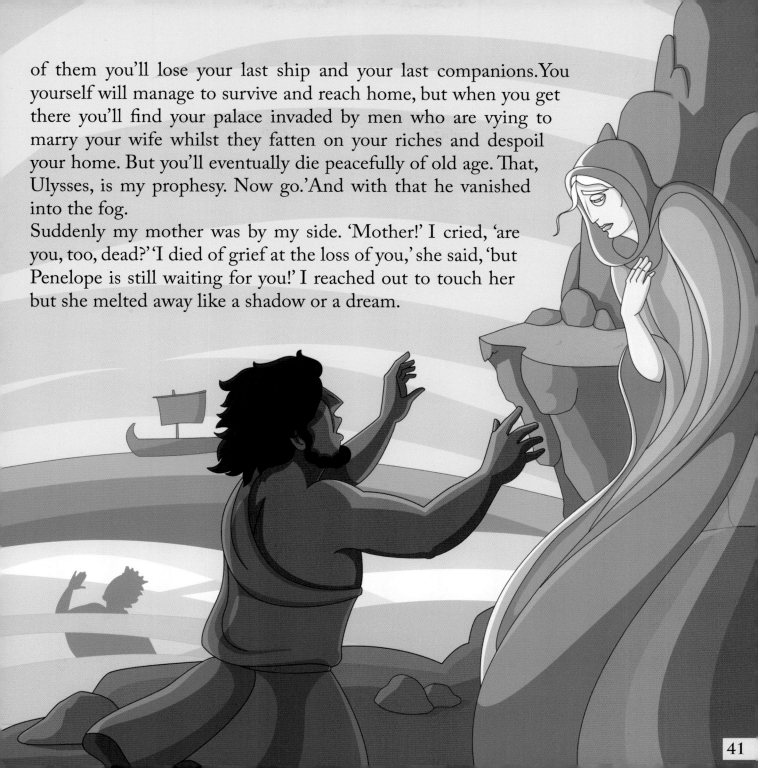

We boarded the ship. For a long time we drifted in the fog but eventually came into clear air, very near the Isle of the Sirens. Circe had warned me not to listen to the sweet song the Sirens sing. 'For if you do you,' she warned earnestly, 'you won't be able to resist a mad desire to land on their shore, where all of you would die. Seal the ears of your men with wax and have them tie you firmly to the mast, with strict orders not to release you no matter how you might rave and rant!' Hardly had the Sirens sighted us but that they intoned their irresistible song and chanted **'Come to us, glorious Ulysses and all you brave men! Beach your ship and join our songs and pleasures!'**

It was utterly irresistible! I shouted at my men and implored them to untie me and let me swim ashore, but what with their ears being plugged they heard neither the Sirens nor my antics and stayed faithful to my orders; and so we passed the Sirens safe and sound.

Not many days later the sea began to roil up. Before us loomed two enormous cliffs in the midst of wild crashing breakers. Circe had warned me: 'You'll have to pass through the straits between two huge cliffs with open-mouthed caves in their fronts. There dwell the monsters Scylla and Charybdis. Charybdis thrice a day sucks in enormous amounts of water and with it anything afloat on it; and Scylla, a repulsive creature with six heads on long snake-like necks, grabs and devours everything she can reach. If you sail close to Charybdis, your ship will be sucked into the terrible whirlpool, and if close to Scylla you'll lose six men. But it's surely better to sacrifice these than for the whole lot of you to perish . . .'

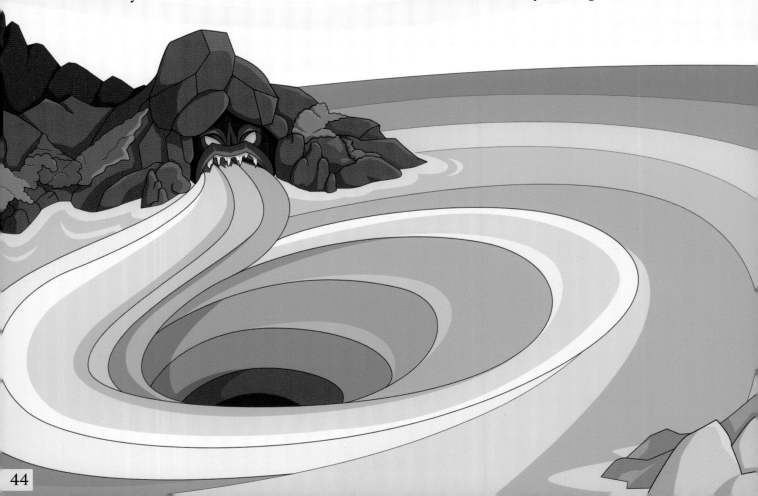

And so it came about. Whilst we kept clear of Charybdis, Scylla's six heads sprung out of the cave, snatched six men off the deck and devoured them. We came through the strait after that, in mourning for our lost mates but once again on the way home. Thus we came to the Isle of the sun god Helios.

Mindful of Teiresias' warning, I wanted to pass by without landing, but Eurylocus and others implored me: 'You're cruel, Ulysses! We're all half dead with fatigue, hunger and thirst . . . let's go ashore at least for the night!'

'All right,' I nodded. 'But you'll have to swear to me that you'll not touch a hair of any of the cows that roam all over the island. **They belong to Hyperion, father of the sun god Helios, and if we harm any of them, Helios will see to it that we all perish horribly.**

'Why would we kill a sacred cow?' asked Eurylocus. 'We'll only stay a day and we have enough provisions of our own.' They all swore to obey me, went ashore and started to prepare the evening meal.

During the night, storm clouds gathered and winds began to howl. That lasted for a day, then for a second day and for a third, and eventually for a month. Neither sea nor wind seemed to want to calm down. Our reserved of food ran out and the men became desperate. Then one day, as I was coming back ashore from the ship, I saw them standing around a cow carcass roasting on a spit over a huge bed of coals. **'Have you all lost your minds?'** I roared at them. But they went on feasting contentedly – there was enough meat for many days.

Helios' fury wasn't long in coming. No sooner had we put out to sea but that a storm arose the likes of which I had never seen. Monster waves swept away my men one by one, and then smashed the ship to pieces. I clung to a piece of the mast and consigned myself to the will of the waves. After nine days of drifting I was washed up on a beach of Ogygia, where the goddess Calypso received me lovingly but refused to let me go. After seven years, Zeus sent Hermes with orders to let me sail away. And that's how I came to be here among you.

When Ulysses had finished his tale there was general silence. Then Alcinous cleared is throat and said 'Ulysses, you've suffered a great deal. I think the time has come for you to make straight for home. We'll do what we can to help you.' And so it came about that a few days later Ulysses set out for Ithaca on a new ship laden with precious gifts. After a few days he fell into so profound a slumber that he failed to notice where the ship was heading until ran aground gently by itself on a foggy beach. He awoke, cold and stiff, and looked about, but the fog let him see little of the land. 'Only the gods know where I've landed now,' he sighed to himself. 'It might have been better to stay with the Phaecians'.

Then he spied a young shepherd. 'My boy, would you please tell me the name of this land?' he called out. 'Why, yes sir, gladly', the lad said brightly. 'Ithaca.'
Ulysses would have fallen on his knees and kissed the ground for sheer joy, but he didn't want to be recognised. 'I've heard talk about Ithaca back home on Crete' he said, 'but I've never been here before . . .'
'Oh crafty Ulysses!' said the boy, laughing, 'master of intrigue and deception . . . **don't you recognise Athena, daughter of Zeus**, she who stands ever by your side and protects you!?' And so saying she changed into a tall and dazzlingly beautiful woman. 'Now, Ulysses, you must go straight to your palace and drive out the rich, lazy and arrogant suitors who are besieging your wife and plotting against your son. I'll change you into an old beggar so that no one will recognise you.

Then I'll go and call back Telemachus, who's gone to Sparta to look for news of you'. 'Tell me why you, who know all things, didn't simply tell him that I was alive, instead of sending him into far-away horizons?'

'I wanted him to become a man and find his own courage in life,' Athena said gently. 'Yes, the suitors have planned an ambush for him, but don't worry, I'll protect him.' With that she stroked his cheek and he turned into an old beggar in rags.

Near his palace, Ulysses stopped first at the hovel of Eumaeus the old swineherd, who said at once 'Oh poor old man, come into my shed and rest a little! Then you'll tell me who you are . . .'

'Tell me the name of your master here,' Ulysses asked.

'My master was Ulysses, but he went off twenty years ago to fight at Troy and never came back. Now his palace is invaded and besmirched by a horde of villains who devour his goods and want to marry Queen Penelope.'

'I've travelled far and wide, my good friend,' said Ulysses, 'and I can promise you that **Ulysses will soon come home!**'

'I'd like to believe you' sighed Eumaeus, 'but by now Ulysses is dead and the dead don't return. But let's talk of other things – the thought of my poor dead master makes me suffer. Tell me where you come from . . .'

'From Crete' said Ulysses, 'and I too fought at Troy. During the voyage back I lost all my ships and men and suffered many hardships.'

'Then rest now,' said Eumaeus. 'Tonight you may sleep here.'

Ulysses rolled himself into a blanket in a corner and fell asleep.

In the morning he was awakened by the voice of a youth calling Eumaeus.

'Telemachus! My beloved master!' he heard Eumaeus cry out with joy. 'You're back, safe and sound!'. 'Yes, thank you, Eumaeus. And who might this stranger be?' 'A man from wealthy Crete who's suffered ill fate and became very poor'. 'I'd gladly put him up in the palace' said Telemachus, 'but I'm no longer master in my own home. Eumaeus, please run to my mother and tell her I'm back. Meanwhile I'll try to discoverer how the suitors are plotting my death.'

Whilst they were thus speaking, Athena told Ulysses that the time had come to reveal himself onto his son; and so she turned Ulysses back into his own self, strong and vigorous as ever. Telemachus was dumbfounded. 'Are you a god?' he stammered. 'One moment you're an old beggar, the next a nobleman!'

Ulysses, with tears in his eyes, said **'No, Telemachus, I'm not a god. I'm your father!'**
'My father!' cried Telemachus, sobbing. 'How . . . how did you manage to return?'
'The Phaecians made it possible, after my many adventures and misadventures.'
They sat and embraced and wept like two eagles whose eaglets have been stolen
by hunters.

Then Ulysses said 'Now we'll have to clean those swine out of our palace. Tell me, how many of them are there?'

'More than a hundred,' said Telemachus sadly.

'Well then. Go back to the palace now and quietly hide all weapons that might be in sight. Tomorrow I'll show up as the old beggar. But let no one know about me, Telemachus! That's vital to our victory!'

The next day Ulysses, again as the beggar, had Eumaeus lead him to the palace. At the threshold he saw his faithful dog Argus lie cowering in a corner, old and abandoned. On hearing Ulysses' voice, Argus raised his head painfully and wagged his tail.

'That was my master's dog, Argus,' said Eumaeus, 'but now no one takes care of him.' Ulysses nearly wept and wanted to hug the animal. The reunion proved too strong for Argus: he made a weak sound and raised his head once more toward Ulysses, then let it sink slowly to the ground and closed his eyes forever.

In the palace Ulysses was greeted by a storm of insults and rude noises. 'Eumaeus,' cried one of the suitors, 'why this filthy beggar?' Ulysses looked about. Everywhere the tables were laden with bread, meats, honeyed sweets, fruit and jars of wine.

'Come and pass among the tables,' said Telemachus to Ulysses, 'every one of these gentlemen will give you some delicacy.'
'First you accuse us of wasting your property, then you yourself want us to throw it away on that creature!' laughed the suitor Antinoos.

53

While Ulysses wound his way among the tables, Penelope entered the hall. 'I promised you all,' she said, 'to pick my future husband today.

Well, then. I'll marry the man who can bend and string Ulysses' bow and shoot an arrow through the twelve rings that decorate these axe heads set up in a straight row.'

'None of us can bend and string Ulysses' bow' cried Antinoos angrily. 'I was only a child but I remember his strength . . .'

'I'll be the first to try' said Telemachus, 'and if I succeed, none of you will marry my mother and all of you will clear out. Is that understood?' General murmur and nodding of assent.

Telemachus tried three times but failed. Then all the others tried and also failed, one by one.

'May I try, too?' asked Ulysses in a quavering old voice.
'How dare you!' shouted Antinoos, 'miserable wretch, you . . .'
'What are you afraid of?' asked Penelope, 'That this poor ill old man might succeed where all of you failed? Let him try – give him the bow!'
Before anyone was fully aware of it Ulysses had bent and strung the bow.

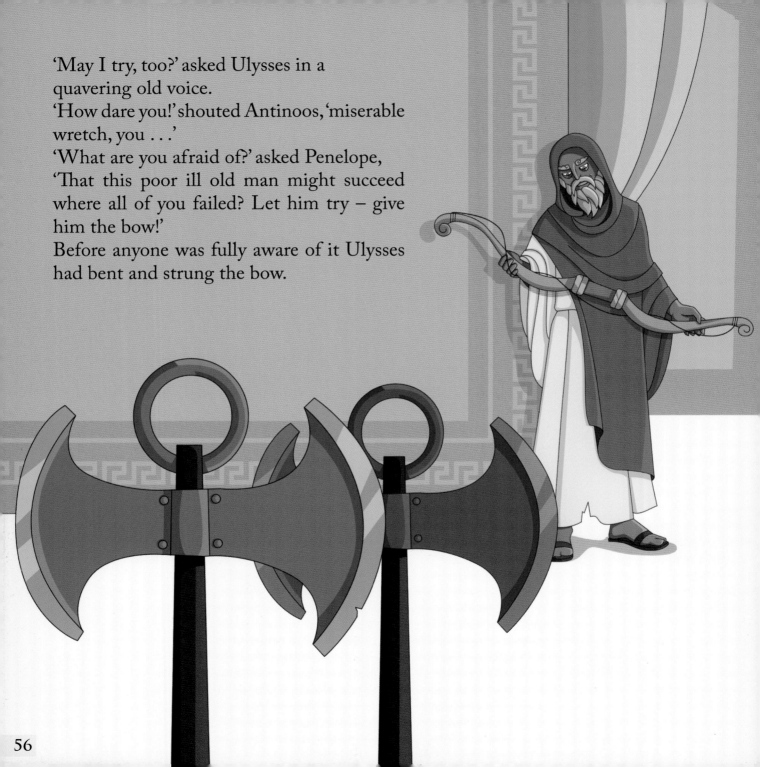

Then he shot an arrow straight through the twelve axe head rings, and at the same moment his figure and rags changed into his true self clad in noble raiment. A second arrow struck Antinoos in the breast so that he crashed to the ground.

'Mangy dogs, did you really think I wouldn't return?' cried Ulysses. 'Prepare to die, all of you!' And so perished one after the other by Ulysses' infallible arrows; not one escaped.

Telemachus turned to his mother. 'Why are you standing there, as though turned to stone? Won't you embrace the husband you haven't seen for twenty years?'

'How can I be certain he really is Ulysses?' She asked, choking with emotion.
'Your mother is right' said Ulysses, who had understood that Penelope was testing him. 'I'm tired and want to sleep.'
'Well then. Servants, bring my wedding bed in here . . .' Penelope ordered.

'That bed' said Ulysses, 'can't be brought anywhere. It's part of the stump of a tree still firmly rooted in the earth. I myself made it.' And so Penelope knew the truth, and they fell into each other's arms laughing and weeping, and stayed long embraced tenderly. During the night Ulysses told Penelope of his adventures. And towards dawn, Athena made them fall into a long deep peaceful sleep.

For Ulysses, the Odyssey was at an end.

In the same series:

DECAMERON I
(Brother Cipolla - Chichibìo - Calandrino and the Heliotrope)

DECAMERON II
(Calandrino and the stolen pig - Costanza and Martuccio)

DANTE FOR FUN - HELL

DANTE FOR FUN - PURGATORY

DANTE FOR FUN - PARADISE

MANZONI FOR FUN - THE BETROTHED

Printed in September 2010
by Federighi Colorgrafiche srl
www.federcol.it

Printed in Italy